# The Tanzania Jum

# Juma Cooks Chapati

## by Lisa Maria Burgess
### illustrated by Abdul M. Gugu

BARRANCA PRESS

**H**ello. My name is Juma. I am Tanzanian.

My *Baba* is from the island of Zanzibar and my *Mama* is from the mainland of Tanzania. Like a little rabbit, I am super quick and full of tricks, so my parents call me *Super Sungura.* But most of the time, I am just Juma— Ijumaa when *Mama* wants to be serious.

Guess what? I like food.

Guess what, what? This morning, I fell out of bed. I was dreaming about food.

When I fall out of bed, I get an idea in my head. Hey, that rhymes. And the idea is so good—Cooking *chapati* all by myself.

Today, since I have to cook *chapati*, I decide to ask the expert to tell me how.

I go to my *Yaya*, who is very nice and makes *chapatis* for me every weekend.

Guess what. She says, "No." She says, "Cooking *chapati* uses lots of hot oil, and you know that hot oil and boys are dangerous together. Go outside."

Guess what, what? I have a plan.

I tell Sareeya – that's my little sister – to crawl on her knees so I can stand on her back by the window. I watch how my *Yaya* pours flour in a bowl and adds water. She lights the fire on the *jiko*.

My sister says, "I'm getting tired and I'm going to fall."

I say, "No. If you fall, I will fall."

She says, "I'm tired."

So I say, "*Little Sungura* – Be strong! How can we make *chapati* if I can't learn the ingredients?"

That *Yaya* hears us arguing. She says, "All right, you crows. Come inside where I can see you."

So we go inside.

Guess what?  My secret plan is to learn the exact steps for making *chapati*.

"We'll help," I say quickly.

My *Yaya* rolls the dough into a pile that looks like coiled snakes.  Then, I roll each dough-snake into a circle, my sister puts oil on the circle, and my *Yaya* cooks and flips and cooks and flips.

Then my sister and I sit on the terrace to eat our *chapatis*—My *Yaya* gives us two each.

Those *chapatis* are good!

We finish eating.

We don't know what to do. "I'm bored," I say.

"Let's play *esta esta*. You find a flat stone and I'll draw the squares," says my sister.

So we play…. Sareeya pushes the stone with her foot while hopping and gets the stone into one square and then the next one.

I follow behind her, hopping on one foot, but I keep falling out of the squares—flat on my bottom.

I say, "This is sooooo boring."

I say, "Let's play *bao* just like *Babu* does with his friends."

We start to dig holes. We dig them two by two until we have six pairs. Two times six, that's twelve holes in the ground. I am very good at mathematics.

We drop three stones into each hole. We take turns dropping stones one by one and scooping up the stones in the last hole. We go around and around.

Finally, we just sit and make piles of dust. That is even more boring.

Then I remember. I have to cook *chapati* by myself. But that *Yaya* is sure to say no—again. She is sure to say, "I'm tidying the house. You do something outside."

Guess what?  I see *Bwana Bustani* at the very back of the garden.

He is raking up old leaves and branches from the trees.

So quick, quick, I sneak into the kitchen and get flour, oil, and salt.  Sareeya brings a bowl, plates, and a fry pan. I go back for water.  I have a good, good plan.

That gardener is my friend.  He helps me when I lose my ball or when I get stuck climbing the coconut palm or in the first branch of the Neem tree.

When I tell him my plan, he laughs and says, "*Sawa.*" I knew he would say okay.  He always helps.

That gardener clears the ground and makes a fire with big branches to hold the fry pan. I mix the flour and oil and salt and water just like my *Yaya* does. Sareeya flattens some dough on a plate with oil. I put the circle of dough in the pan and wait. We are patient. It smells good.

A crow sits in the Neem tree watching us. It says, "Kraaaa." I think maybe Mr. *Kunguru* wants to learn how to make *chapati* too.

My sister says, "It's ready." So I flip. I flip well—it goes up and up.

Guess what? The crow up in the Neem tree sees the *chapati*.

Guess what, what? He flies quick, quick and snap, snap, takes that *chapati* in his beak. Mr. *Kunguru* doesn't want to make *chapati* —

he just wants to eat!

My sister shouts, "That was our *chapati*!"

I say, "*Hakuna shida*. No worries, we can make another one." So we do. This time, before I flip, I make sure the crow is gone.

Just when I start to flip, that gardener calls my name. He says, "Ijumaa, that's hot. You be careful!"

I turn, and instead of flipping up and up, that *chapati* flips sideways—side over side—right into *Bwana Bustani*'s face. It falls in the dirt. First we are surprised and nobody moves. Then we all look at the *chapati* in the dirt. I pick it up.

My sister says, "Can we eat it?"

The gardener says, "No, this is for Mr. *Kunguru* if he is still hungry."

Before my sister starts to shout again, I say, "No worries.  Let's do it again."

So we do.

This time, I don't flip.  When the *chapati* is ready, I turn it with a big fork—*pole, pole*—slowly, slowly.

My sister and I eat that *chapati*.  The *chapati* is very, very good.  Even the gardener says it's good.

Guess what?  We make some more.

Guess what, what?  I'm not bored.

Not one bit.

# Juma's Chapati

**Ingredients:**    1+ cups water

¾ cup cooking oil

1 tsp salt

2 ½ cups flour

**Cooking:**

**1.** Get two small pans and one large bowl.

• In the first small pan, mix 1 cup water, 3 Tablespoons of oil, and 1 tsp salt. Heat until warm.

• In the second small pan, heat ½ cup cooking oil until warm.

• In the large bowl, put 2 ½ cups flour. Add the hot water mixture from the first pan. Mix until the dough forms a smooth ball. Add water as needed.

**2.** Pinch off a small ball of dough.

**3.** Using a rolling pin, flatten the ball into a circle. Brush the circle of dough with warm oil.

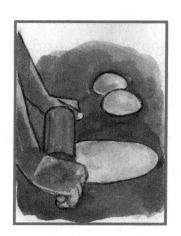

**4.** Roll the circle of dough into a snake and coil. Set aside and repeat the process until the dough is finished.

**5.** Flatten each coiled snake of dough and roll into a circle with the rolling pin.

**6.** Cook on a hot griddle, turning so that both sides are cooked to golden. You can brush the dough with more warm oil and turn— this will soften the chapati.

This recipe makes about eight chapatis.

# Dar es Salaam

Juma's family lives in Dar es Salaam, the economic capital of Tanzania.

The city is very big and is spread along the coast of the Indian Ocean.
At the centre of the city is the harbour. The main districts are Kinondoni,
Ilala, and Temeke. The family's house is in the neighbourhood of Tabata.

AFRICA

Indian
Ocean

Tanzania

Atlantic
Ocean

## Ki-Swahili and English Glossary:

| | |
|---|---|
| *Baba:* | Father |
| *Babu:* | Grandfather |
| *Bao:* | Game played with small round stones in a series of 12 holes |
| *Bwana Bustani:* | Mr. Gardener |
| *Chapati:* | Flat bread similar to the Mexican tortilla or the Indian roti |
| *Esta esta:* | Children's game similar to hopscotch |
| *Hakuna shida:* | No worries |
| *Jiko:* | Small stove |
| *Kunguru:* | Crow |
| *Mama:* | Mother |
| *Pole pole:* | Slowly, slowly |
| *Sawa:* | Okay |
| *Sungura:* | Rabbit |
| *Yaya:* | Nanny |

## About the Authors:

At the time of writing these stories, **Lisa Maria Burgess** taught in the Department of Literature at the University of Dar es Salaam. She wrote the Juma stories with her sons, **Matoko** and **Senafa**.

## About the Illustrator:

**Abdul M. Gugu** lives in Dar es Salaam where he works as an illustrator of children's books and as an artist.

www.barrancapress.com


FIRST EDITION, July 2013




ISBN  978-1-939604-04-0




Library of Congress Catalog Card Number:  2013937630




Manufactured in the United States of America.

CPSIA information can be obtained at www.ICGtesting.com
Printed in the USA
LVOW020738050713

341496LV00001B/1/P